Let's Dance

Carmel Reilly

Australia • Brazil • Japan • Korea • Mexico • Singapore • Spain • United Kingdom • United States

Let's Dance

Fast Forward
Blue Level 9

Text: Carmel Reilly
Illustrations: Christina Miesen
Editor: Kate McGough
Design: James Lowe
Series design: James Lowe
Production controller: Emma Hayes
Photo research: Michelle Cottrill
Audio recordings: Juliet Hill, Picture Start
Spoken by: Matthew King and Abbe Holmes

Acknowledgements
The author and publisher would like to acknowledge permission to reproduce material from the following sources: Photographs by AAP Image/ Mark J. Terrill, p 14 bottom; Alamy/ Tim Graham, p 8; Fairfax Photos/ Robert Pearce, p 13 top; Getty Images/ News and Sport, pp 9, 10, 14 top/ Reportage, p 13 bottom/ Stone, p 15 bottom/ Taxi, front cover, pp 1, 15 top; Newspix/ Bill Mcauley, p 12/ Jim Alcorn, p 11/ John Grainger, p 7 top/ Rohan Kelly, p 5; Reuters, p 7 bottom; Wildlight/ Penny Tweedie, p 4.

ISBN 978 0 17 012530 7
ISBN 978 0 17 012525 3 (set)

Cengage Learning Australia
Level 7, 80 Dorcas Street
South Melbourne, Victoria Australia 3205
Phone: 1300 790 853

Cengage Learning New Zealand
Unit 4B Rosedale Office Park
331 Rosedale Road, Albany, North Shore NZ 0632
Phone: 0508 635 766

For learning solutions, visit cengage.com.au

Printed in China by 1010 Printing International Ltd
2 3 4 5 6 7 8 12 11 10 09 08

THE UNIVERSITY OF
MELBOURNE

Evaluated in independent research by staff from the Department of Language, Literacy and Arts Education at the University of Melbourne.

Let's Dance

Carmel Reilly

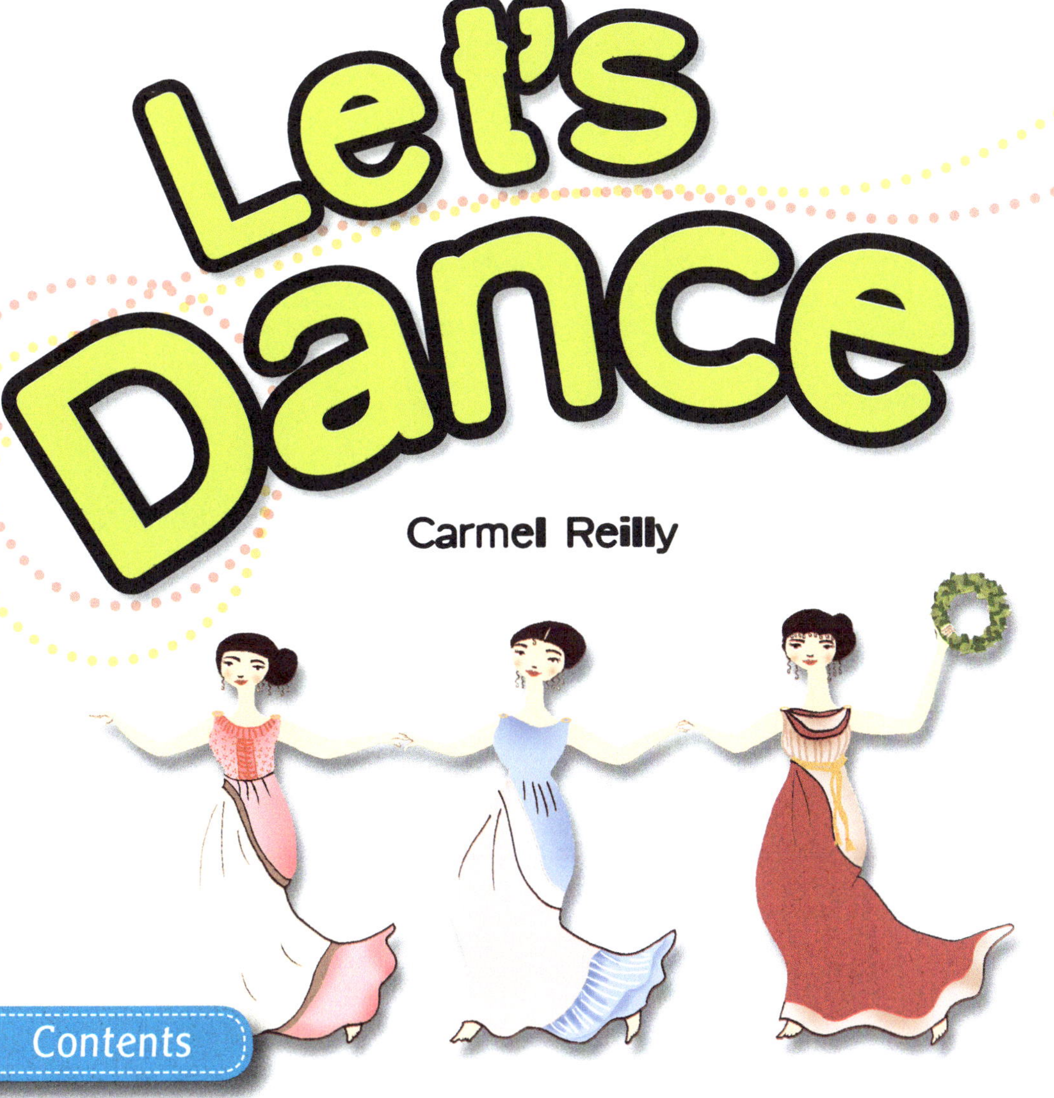

Contents

DANCE

Dance is a very old art form.
It has been a part of people's lives for a very long time.

Why Do People Dance?

People dance:

- to **celebrate**
- as part of a **ritual**
- to tell a story
- as a **performance** art form
- for something fun to do
- for a mix of these things!

TURN
STEP

CELEBRATING WITH DANCE

Dances are used to celebrate different things.

In old times, people celebrated the coming of a new baby or having a good harvest.

Today, Chinese people celebrate their New Year with a lion dance.

Dance is also a big part of celebrating New Year in parts of India.

RITUALS

Dances can be part of a ritual.

In New Zealand, Maori warriors danced the haka as a ritual before going to war. Doing the haka made the warriors feel strong.

Running Words 127

Today, New Zealand sports teams dance the haka to help them feel strong before they play a game.

The haka is also danced by New Zealand soldiers before they go to war.

Chapter 4

TELLING STORIES

Some **cultures** use dance to tell stories.

In Australia, Aboriginal people use dance to tell dreaming stories.
These dances are one of the ways that Aboriginal people can remember their dreaming stories, and pass them on to their children.

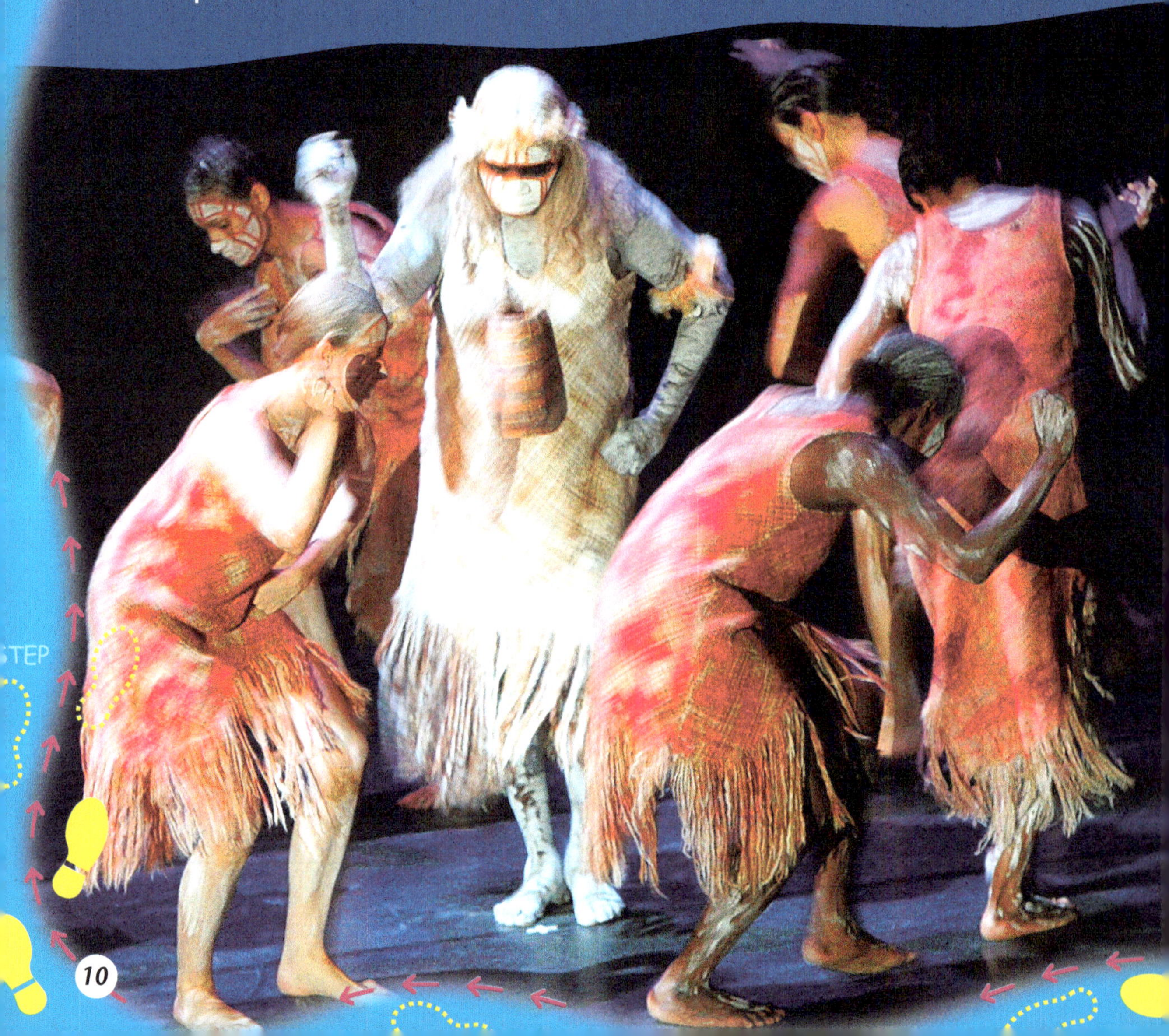

Dreaming stories are about how the world and the people and animals in it came to be.

Chapter 5

PERFORMANCE ART

In some countries, dances have been made into a performance art form that only a few people can do. Ballet is one of these dances.

Ballet dancers have to be very strong and fit.
It takes them years of hard work to be really good.

Countries, like India and China,
have special performance dances, too.
These are also very hard to do and take years to learn.

Chapter 6

HAVING FUN

There are lots of dances that everyone can do. Some take time to learn the right moves, like hip hop dancing.

But, for lots of people,
dance is just about getting up
and moving to the music.
Dance is about having a good time
with friends.
Dance is about having fun.

Glossary

celebrate to have fun at a special event

cultures groups of people from different places around the world, with their own kinds of food, art and ideas about the world

performance something that is done by one person or a group of people, in front of an audience

ritual something that is always done in a special way at special times, like a dance that is only performed at New Year each year

Index